# Dunc and the Flaming Ghost

# Gary Paulsen

## Dunc and the Flaming Ghost

A YEARLING BOOK

Published by
Dell Publishing
a division of
Bantam Doubleday Dell Publishing Group, Inc.
666 Fifth Avenue
New York, New York 10103

ISBN: 0-440-40686-2

Printed in the United States of America

December 1992

10 9 8 7 6 5 4 3 2 1

OPM

# Dunc and the Flaming Ghost

# Chapter · 1

Duncan—Dunc—Culpepper sat on his bicycle in front of the old Rambridge house beside his best friend for life, Amos Binder. Amos stared at the house's front door with a frown.

"Are you going to go in and get him?" Dunc asked.

"No way."

Amos's dog, Scruff, had just disappeared into the house.

"All I did was try to pet him," Amos said.

"Why doesn't he like you?"

Amos scratched his head. "How would the school counselor put it? The sharp

**1**

chasm between our personalities is difficult to breach."

Dunc balanced in place on his bicycle. He was pretty good at it. "So why don't you just go in and get him?"

"Haven't you ever heard the story about Old Man Caruthers?"

"Who's Old Man Caruthers?"

"There's a legend that says Blackbeard the Pirate hid millions in jewels somewhere around here," Amos said. "Old Man Caruthers used to brag that he knew where the treasure was. One night about twenty years ago he broke into the Rambridge house to get it."

"What happened?"

"No one really knows. The neighbors said they heard him scream, then there was a real low, evil laugh. His scream was cut off short, just like you cut a piece of meat with a cleaver." Amos ran his finger across his throat. He shuddered.

Dunc straightened out his handlebars. He was still balancing. "So did they ever find Caruthers's body?"

"No. Some say he died in the cellar, others in the bedroom. Almost everybody says it was Blackbeard's ghost that killed him."

"Blackbeard's ghost?"

"Yeah." Amos shuddered again.

Dunc shook his head. "I don't believe it."

"Why not?"

"Because I don't believe in ghosts, that's why." He set his feet down on the sidewalk. "You'll still have to go in and get Scruff. You can't leave that poor dog in there all night."

Amos looked at the house. It was old and falling apart. The paint had peeled off, and all the boards were bleached a grayish white. The last rays of the sun behind it made it look even spookier. If there was anyplace a ghost would want to live, the Rambridge house was it.

"Maybe he hid in there because he wants it to be his new home," Amos said. "Maybe he and Blackbeard get along really well, a kind of boy-and-his-dog type of thing."

"But he's your dog."

"Blackbeard can keep Scruff. Scruff never liked me anyway."

"You don't mean that. Your sister would be heartbroken."

"Then she can go in after him. Blackbeard can keep her, too. Or my grandparents, or Mom and Dad, or Melissa—" He stopped. "Well, maybe not her." Amos was in love with a girl named Melissa Hansen.

Dunc climbed off his bike. "C'mon."

"C'mon where?"

"We're going to get Scruff." He grabbed Amos's arm and dragged him toward the front door.

"What do you mean, 'we'? Why does it have to be 'we'? Why can't you do it yourself?"

"Because you need to get over this silly superstition about ghosts."

"But I like superstitions. There's nothing wrong with a good, healthy superstition once in a while."

Dunc wasn't listening to him. He had Amos halfway to the front door.

"I'll tell you what," Amos pleaded. "If you go in and get Scruff, you can have him. Free."

"What would your sister say?"

"Just don't bring him over to the house. I'll tell her a dump truck ran over him."

Dunc almost had to carry Amos up the front steps into the house.

Inside, it was like midnight. Just enough light was coming through the dusty windows to outline an old fireplace crouched against one wall with a picture hanging above it. There wasn't any furniture and absolutely nothing that resembled a ghost.

The picture was of an old man with piercing black eyes. "That must be Mr. Rambridge," Dunc said.

"I don't care. I don't like it in here."

"This isn't so bad. It's just an old house."

"All haunted houses are old."

"You don't really think this place is haunted, do you?"

"The thought has crossed my mind." Amos crossed his fingers and held them out in front of him. All the movies said crosses kept ghosts away. Or maybe it was vampires. Either way, he wasn't going to take any chances.

"Even if it was, what could a ghost do to you? Punch you a good one? His hand would go right through your face. Big deal."

"We're not talking about any old ghost.

**5**

We're talking about the ghost of Black-beard. I've heard he used to make people chew the insides of their cheeks off and blow bubbles with them like gum."

"The only thing we need to worry about is these rotten floorboards. They could collapse at any moment."

"And Blackbeard would get us. He's probably waiting under them for us right now." Amos flashed his crossed fingers at the floor.

"Will you relax?" Dunc studied the room. "Do you have any idea how old this place is?"

"I don't care."

"There aren't any wall outlets. It must have been built before electricity. I bet there isn't any internal plumbing, either—maybe just a hand pump in the sink. Let's see if we can find the kitchen."

Amos grabbed his shoulder before he had a chance to wander off. "No. Let's just find Scruff and get out of here."

"Are you really afraid?"

"I just want to get out of here."

Dunc shrugged his shoulders. "All right. Stay close."

He didn't have to say that. Amos was draped over his back like a cloak.

"What are you doing?"

"Staying close. You said to stay close."

"You don't have to stay *that* close."

"I just want to be sure I don't lose you."

Dunc studied the room again. "If you were Scruff, where would you be?"

"Upstairs. Every time I come in the house, Scruff growls and hides under my sister's bed."

"I don't see a staircase," Dunc said. "Wait, there it is."

He pointed toward an old wooden case with an ornately carved banister. It climbed the far wall and ended at a doorway on the second floor.

"Let's go." He led Amos across the room.

"If you see a ghost, you'll tell me, won't you?"

"There are no such things."

"Tell me anyway. I don't want to get my head cut off just because you say there are no such things."

7

Dunc ignored him.

"If we see a ghost," Amos said, "so long, Scruff. I don't care how heartbroken my sister is. I don't care if she cries herself to sleep and drowns in her soggy pillow."

"We're not going to see a ghost. Be careful going up these stairs. Make sure you step on the sides and not in the middle in case the boards are rotten. You go first." He pushed Amos up the first step. It creaked loudly.

"Here, doggy," Amos tried to call. He was so scared, his voice squeaked. He stepped onto the second step. It creaked worse than the first. Dunc followed him.

"Here, Scruff old boy."

Scruff came out on the landing above them. He took one look at Amos, growled, and trotted back into the darkness.

"There he is," Amos said. "I'll just go up and—" He stopped. "Do you smell something burning?"

"Burning?" Dunc sniffed. "Yeah, I do. What is it?"

"Don't ask me."

**8**

*"Why don't you ask me?"* a loud voice boomed.

A light appeared suddenly at the top of the stairs. Amos and Dunc froze. Solid.

They heard heavy footsteps like thunder. When they looked up, they saw a huge man carrying a lantern. He was glowing white and had a hat pulled down over thick, greasy hair, and two lit matches, one sticking out of each side of his head. He looked at them and laughed. The laugh sounded like somebody breaking bones with an ax.

*"Why don't you ask me?"* He bellowed again.

And the boys were gone.


Dunc didn't know how he made it outside, but his feet never touched the floor.

Amos didn't know how he made it, either. The only thing that Amos's feet touched was Dunc's back as he ran over him on his way down the stairs.

They burst out the front door like an explosion, screaming and tripping over each other. They hurdled the fence that encircled the yard and collapsed on the sidewalk, panting and scared spitless.

Scruff trotted out after them, his tongue wagging out of the side of his mouth. When he reached the fence he cocked his head to one side and looked at them curiously.

Amos stared at Dunc. He took a deep breath, took another one without exhaling, then one more, and screamed directly into Dunc's ear:

"Now do you believe in ghosts?"

# Chapter · 2

"It couldn't have been a ghost," Dunc said.

He and Amos were sitting at a table in the school library. It was that point in the afternoon when they began thinking less and less about schoolwork and more and more about other things. They were supposed to be working on book reports.

"I don't want to talk about it. I don't want to even think about it. We're supposed to be studying."

"But it *couldn't* have been a ghost. It's just not possible."

"You didn't seem so convinced about that last night." Amos snorted. "I barely caught

**11**

up with you. That reminds me—how's your back?"

Dunc squirmed. "It's all right, I guess." He had a big bruise in the shape of a footprint right between his shoulder blades.

"It's amazing you could run as fast as you did with a bruise like that. You must have broken eight or ten land speed records. If you had cleats on and a track coach saw you, you'd be in the Olympics." He shook his head. "And now you say what we saw last night couldn't have been a ghost."

"I didn't have time to think about it last night."

"What's to think about? It was huge and white. It had matches sticking out of its head. It was either someone with a serious skin disorder and mental problems, or it was the ghost of Captain Edward Teach. In either case it doesn't matter. I just about peed my pants."

"Who was that?" Dunc asked. "The name you mentioned?"

"Edward Teach. Blackbeard the Pirate. He used to stick matches under the brim of his hat to look scarier. Personally, I don't think he needed them."

"How do you know about Blackbeard?"

"I looked him up in the encyclopedia."

"It just isn't possible."

"Sure it is. You just look under *B,* and there it is. You read about it, and then you know about it."

"I don't mean that. It just isn't possible that what we saw was Blackbeard's ghost."

Amos sighed. "When are you going to admit you don't know everything? There are some things people just aren't meant to understand. Ghosts are one of them."

"I still don't think—"

He stopped in midsentence. Amos had just kicked him under the table.

"What did you do that for?"

"Melissa. Melissa just came in the library."

Dunc looked over his shoulder. Melissa was walking with one of her friends between two bookshelves.

"So?"

"What do you mean, 'so'? This could be

my big opportunity. Watch this." He stood up and sauntered over to the aisle.

*He's being cool,* Dunc thought. *That's not good.*

Amos pretended he didn't know Melissa was there. He took a book off the shelf and opened it.

*Here it comes,* Dunc thought.

Amos leaned his free hand against a row of books. There was no backing behind them, and they shot out into the adjacent aisle like cannonballs. They hit the librarian right in the nose as she was reshelving a book about human anatomy. She was out cold, with her glasses split down the middle and hanging from her ears.

Amos lost his balance and clutched the shelf as he fell. It broke off in his hand and tumbled to the ground with him. An avalanche of books about skiing cascaded down, burying him. Only his feet stuck out from under the pile. Melissa looked at him and shook her head. As he climbed to his feet, she walked away.

After the mess was cleaned up and the

school nurse had led the dazed librarian away, Amos walked back to the table.

"I don't think that went too well," Amos said. "What do you think?"

"Amos—"

"You're right. Melissa must think I'm a real dork now."

"I wouldn't worry about that. A book about the Alps fell on your head. I don't think she recognized you."

"Good. Then she still thinks I'm cool."

"Well—"

"What were we talking about?" Amos snapped his fingers. "I remember. Ghosts. You said ghosts couldn't exist because they don't fit your narrow way of thinking."

"That isn't what I said. I said it wasn't possible for *this* ghost to exist."

"Why not?"

"Since when do ghosts have to use doorways? I thought they could walk through walls."

"They don't always have to walk through walls. I imagine that if they want to use doorways, they can."

"Since when do ghosts need to carry lan-

**15**

terns or clomp their feet on stairways? If he was a ghost, how could he clomp his feet at all?"

"Ghosts have been known to carry lights. They've also been known to make noises."

"So have people. In fact, I'd say the vast majority of all beings who have to carry lights, make noise, and use doorways are people."

"Are you saying that ghost was a man dressed up like a ghost?"

"That's exactly what I'm saying."

"Why would he do that?"

"I don't know. Maybe there's something in the house he's trying to hide."

"Or maybe he's a ghost and he gets a big kick out of scaring people. Maybe he wants to scare them to death so he has some company."

"There's only one way to find out."

Amos leaned back in the library chair. "No way, Dunc. Uh-uh. Not for all the money in the world."

"Come on, Amos. Maybe Blackbeard's treasure really is in the house. Maybe the man's protecting it."

"Treasure. You always say there might be treasure, but there never is. We find gunpowder exploding and time warps closing, but we never find any treasure."

"But why else would he want to scare us away?"

"Because he's a ghost and it's his nature."

"I bet Melissa would be impressed if you went back in again. She'd think you were brave."

"She already thinks I'm cool. She doesn't need to think I'm brave."

"But she'll love you forever."

"Don't bring her into this. You always sucker me into things by bringing in Melissa."

"Well, all right, if you don't want to even try. I just thought . . ." Dunc shrugged. "Forget it."

Amos watched him for a long time. Dunc was reading his book. He didn't look up.

"Forget what?"

"Nothing. It's silly."

"Tell me, Dunc."

"It's just a stupid idea I had. It's not worth bringing up."

"Are you going to tell me, or do I have to jump over the table and shake it out of you?"

Dunc closed his book. "All right, if you really want to know."

"I want to know."

"I was just thinking that if we found the treasure, we'd get our picture in the paper. Women always go for guys who get their picture in the paper."

"Do they?"

"Sure. I know Melissa does, anyway. She cuts out pictures of one guy and puts them on her wall every time he's in the paper."

"Who?"

"Biff Fastrack."

"Biff Fastrack?" Biff was the captain of the football team. He scored a million touchdowns a game or something. "Melissa likes Biff? He doesn't have a neck."

"The only reason she likes him is because he gets his picture in the paper."

"It would have to be. How can a girl like

**18**

someone who doesn't have a neck? It would be like falling in love with Barney Rubble."

"On the other hand, you have a neck . . ."

"And if I can get my picture in the paper . . ."

The bell rang. School was over.

"Let's go," Amos said.

"Where to?"

"Over to your house. We have to plan how we're going to investigate the Rambridge house."

# Chapter · 3

"Listen," Amos said. "I'm having second thoughts about this."

He and Dunc were lying in the grass on top of a hill overlooking the back of the Rambridge house. Dunc had a pair of binoculars and was trying to look through a window.

"Think about your picture on Melissa's wall," he said.

Amos thought. "Well . . ."

"When we find this treasure, it will probably be the size of the whole front page."

"Kind of like a poster, huh?"

"She could laminate it. That way she could kiss it without ruining the paper."

"Let's go," Amos said.

"Go where?"

"Into the house. We'll never see anything from up here. If you want to see ghosts, you have to go in and see them. I've been by this house a million times and never seen a thing."

"What time of the day did you go by?" Dunc asked.

"All times of the day."

"Ever watch it at night?"

"Yes. I ran by here last Halloween at the stroke of midnight, after I left your place. I didn't see a single ghost."

"Do you want to know why?" Dunc asked.

"I already know why. Ghosts don't care what their neighbors are doing, so you don't see them peeking out the windows."

"That's not the reason. The reason is that there are no such things as ghosts."

"Tell that to the big white guy with the smoking ears." Amos pulled up a blade of grass and chewed on it.

"What side of the house did you run by?" Dunc asked.

"The front side."

"Ever watch the back?"

"Well . . . no."

"Good. Then we're not wasting our time." He put the binoculars down. "I can't see anything—"

"I told you."

"—yet. We'll just have to wait a little longer. Something's bound to happen."

"How can you be so sure?"

"Look at the gravel road that runs along the back. See those tire tracks? Somebody must have been driving there not too long ago, or the rain would've washed the tracks away. Ghosts don't drive vehicles."

"Don't be so sure. I heard a story once about a truck driver who ran himself off a cliff instead of hitting a school bus, and now hitchhikers on that road say they get picked up by a spooky trucker with big green eyes."

"Look." Dunc pointed down the hill. "I told you we wouldn't have to wait long."

A white van drove down the gravel road. It stopped behind the Rambridge house, and two men climbed out. One of them with a bottle in his hand unlocked the back door. The other walked to the rear of the van and took out a large box. He followed the first man into the house.

"I wonder what's in that box," Dunc said.

"A ghost cage."

"How do you know that?"

"I've seen them on Saturday-morning cartoons. A box that size could hold a thousand ghosts. You can pack them in like sardines."

"Let's go down and find out."

"Now? With those two down there?"

"We'll wait a little while and see if they leave and, if they do, whether the box goes with them." Dunc studied the house with the binoculars again.

Minutes passed. The minutes turned into an hour, then two hours. Dunc was still studying the house. Amos was watching the sun begin to set. The rays looked like the light in Melissa's hair when the sun hit it. He tried to imagine the two of them running through the fields, romantic music in the air, their arms outstretched to each other.

But every time he did, he saw himself tripping on something. Even his imagination was clumsy.

"This is boring, Dunc."

"Have patience. Something will happen."

"We've been waiting for two hours for something to happen. Nothing has. Nothing will."

"Those guys went in. They have to come out again." A bead of sweat rolled down Dunc's face. He wiped it away without taking his eyes from the binoculars. He stiffened.

"Here they come," he said.

The two men came out the back door. They climbed into the van and drove away.

Dunc stood up. "Let's go."

"Go where?"

"Down to the house."

"They didn't take the box with them. That means there's a thousand ghosts in there, not to mention Blackbeard."

"Well, I'm going." Dunc jogged down the hill.

Amos didn't move. He shook his head. "It isn't worth it. No newspaper will put a picture on the front page of a guy with chewed-off cheeks. I don't want to face a ghost."

He was talking to himself. Dunc was already halfway down the hill. Amos stood and reluctantly followed.

# Chapter · 4

"The door's locked."

Dunc scanned the back of the house. There were no other doors and no windows they could reach. "We'll have to go in the front."

Amos stared at him. "Don't you remember the last time we tried going in the front? We ran into Blackbeard, and—"

"I already told you. One of those two guys in the van was Blackbeard."

"You don't know that."

"One of them had to be." Dunc walked around the side of the house. Amos could see there was no point in trying to stop him.

It was already dark inside. The house looked almost the same as it had the night before, except there was no ghost at the top of the stairs.

*Yet,* Amos thought.

There wasn't a ghost there yet. To make him blow bubbles with his cheeks. Or worse. Yet.

He stopped just inside the door. "I don't see anything, do you? Good. Let's go." He took two steps, then Dunc grabbed him by the back of his collar.

"You're choking me, Dunc!"

"Sorry." He let go. "I didn't mean to. It's just that we've come too far to give up now."

"That's a matter of opinion."

Dunc ignored him. "That box must be upstairs."

"Why?"

"Because that's where the ghost tried to keep us from going last night."

"There"—Amos nodded—"you called him a ghost. Right there. You actually did it. Let's go. Now."

"Come on." Dunc moved toward the

staircase. Halfway across the living room, Amos stopped him.

"What?"

"Do you smell something burning?"

Dunc sniffed. "No."

"I do. It smells like matches. Ghost matches."

"Amos, don't be ridiculous. I already told you—"

They heard footsteps on the landing above them.

"Run!" Amos gasped.

"No. Let's wait a minute."

Amos wanted to run, but he stopped, waiting. He put his hands over his eyes—he'd read that you turned to stone or salt or mayonnaise or something if you looked directly at them. But he couldn't keep from peeking between his fingers. He saw a glow coming from the door.

Suddenly the ghost stepped onto the landing, the two sides of his head burning ghastly white. He saw them and raised his lantern.

*"Get out."*

Amos grabbed Dunc's shoulder. "That's a good idea, Dunc. Let's go."

"This isn't possible," Dunc said. "He can't exist."

"I don't care. I'm taking his advice." Amos tried to run, but his knees wouldn't bend. Neither would his fingers. Or his tongue. He was scared stiff.

*"Get out,"* the ghost repeated. He trudged down the creaking stairs.

Amos tried to oblige him, but he couldn't lift his feet off the floor. He ran his tongue along the inside of his cheek.

It was a little gummy, he thought. Maybe with some sugar . . .

He finally forced his feet to move, just barely. But as he dragged them toward the door, his heel caught on a loose floorboard. He fell, dragging Dunc down with him. The ghost was halfway down the stairs.

"Kill . . ." Amos groaned, trying to crawl out from beneath Dunc. "Dead . . . us . . ."

"No, he won't."

"Pirates, broadswords, cuts," Amos hissed. "Torture, bubbles, big red bubbles."

"Why would he kill us? What have we—"

At that moment the step underneath the ghost's right foot caved in. He hung in the air for a moment, teetering, then fell forward with a sound like a tree coming down. He landed in a heap at the foot of the stairs.

# Chapter · 5

"Why me? Why always me?"

The ghost climbed to his feet and sat on the bottom stair. He pulled the matches out of the brim of his hat and held his head in his hands.

"Are you all right?" Dunc asked. He and Amos still sat in the middle of the floor, watching him.

"I just fell down the stairs, and my knee hurts, and I bruised my elbow and singed my ear with a match, and you ask me if I'm all right?"

"Who are you?"

"Who do I look like?"

"You look like Blackbeard."

"I do?" The ghost's face brightened. "Thank you. That's who I was trying to look like."

"Trying to? You mean you're not?"

"Me—Blackbeard?" The ghost laughed. "Of course not! Blackbeard would never have fallen down the stairs. He would have been able to scare people out of his home. Any ghost should be able to do that, don't you think?"

"I think so."

"Of course! But I can't. I'm a failure." He shook his head again.

"What's your name?" Amos asked.

"Eddie."

"Eddie?" He looked at Dunc.

"Is there something wrong with that name?" the ghost asked.

"I thought ghosts were supposed to have big, evil-sounding names. Eddie is kind of, well . . . tame."

"It's not my fault. That's what my parents named me. And I never said I was a ghost."

Dunc climbed to his feet. "You're not?"

"Don't be silly. Of course not. There's no such things as ghosts."

Amos stood up, too. "You look like a ghost."

"Don't try to flatter me."

"I mean it."

"Really?" His face brightened again. "Thank you."

"Why are you doing this?"

Eddie sighed. "I found this nice old house to live in that nobody wants, and to keep people from constantly bothering me, I decided I'd play ghost until everyone was scared away. But you can see how good I am at that. No, I can't do anything right." He put his head in his hands again.

Eddie looked a little more human up close than he did at the top of the stairs.

"How'd you get so white?" Amos asked.

"Makeup."

"Why would you want to live in an old rickety house like this?" Dunc asked.

"I can afford it."

"What do you do for a living?"

"I used to be a schoolteacher, but they fired me for whispering and passing notes

**35**

in class." He stuck his chin out. "Now," he said with dignity, "I am a gentleman of leisure."

Amos looked at Dunc. "A bum."

Eddie stood up and paced back and forth across the floor, testing his knee. He limped a little.

"All I wanted was a place where no one would bother me. Now everyone in town will know about the old crazy guy at the Rambridge house pretending to be Blackbeard's ghost. I'll never have a moment's peace."

"We won't tell anyone," Dunc said.

"You won't?"

"No. If no one else is using this place, why shouldn't you?"

"That's the problem." Eddie sat back down on the stair. "Somebody else *is* using it."

"What do you mean?"

"Well—" The stair groaned loudly once, then snapped in half. Eddie fell through. He looked like a white pretzel with two ends sticking in the air, wiggling. Amos and Dunc had to help him up.

Eddie clenched his teeth, reached behind, and jerked. "Splinter," he said, his
breath whistling. "I hate this—if I'm not
falling down the stairs, I'm getting splinters
in my butt. I'm just not having a very good
day."

"What do you mean, somebody else is using the house?" Dunc repeated.

"I can hear them prowling around in the
cellar." He rubbed his behind. "I don't know
what they're doing."

"Why don't you try to scare them off?"

"Because they aren't two boys frightened
of their own shadows. They're big, rough
men. They have to be."

"Why do you say that?"

"Because they go down in the cellar."

"So?"

"There are . . . things down there." Eddie shuddered.

"What kind of things?" Dunc asked.

"Things that make noises in the night.
Big noises. Clunking and pulling and dragging and rattling noises."

"And you still want to live here?"

"I live upstairs. They stay in the basement and don't bother me."

"That wouldn't be a good enough reason for me to live here," Amos said. "In fact, I might just leave the city—even the state. I'm going to grow up, buy a car, marry Melissa, and leave. Tomorrow."

"Amos—"

"Or maybe the whole country. I'll have to find another one. Do they have ghosts in England?"

"Millions," Dunc said. "That's the worst place for them."

"Then I'll go to Antarctica. The worst thing there would be ghost penguins."

Dunc shook his head. "First of all, we don't know if the noises are really ghosts—"

"I do," Amos said. "I know it."

"—and if the men can go down in the cellar, they can't be all that scary. Let's have a look."

"You're nuts."

"Amos, the men brought the box down there. Don't you want to find out what's in it?"

"Not if it means running into dead things that still move around."

"Noises," Eddie corrected. "Dead noises."

"Okay. Dead noises that still move around."

But Dunc was gone, headed for the back of the house where a stairway led down from the kitchen.

"I hate that," Amos said to Eddie.

"What?"

"When he just leaves like that. I hate that. He knows I'll follow him and I always do follow him, and I just hate that."

He followed Dunc.

# Chapter · 6

From the top of the stairs the cellar looked like a bottomless pit. The light from Eddie's lantern didn't seem to illuminate very much.

"Do you see anything?" Dunc asked.

"Nothing," Amos said, "and I prefer to keep it that way."

"Go down the steps a little farther."

"Are you crazy?"

Dunc sighed. "I guess I'll have to find the box myself. I'll get all the credit, all the glory. My picture will be on Melissa's wall."

Amos led the way down the stairs.

The lantern light showed what looked

like a typical cellar. All the walls were made of brick except the far wooden one. There were shelves filled with old boxes, jars, and wine bottles. Everything was dusty. It looked as if no one had been down there in fifty years.

"Look at the floor," Dunc said.

There were footprints in the dust leading to the wooden wall.

"The two men in the van. It's their tracks. See how they lead from the door to the wooden wall and back again?" He rapped the wood with his knuckles. It sounded hollow.

"I bet it's a secret door," Eddie said.

"I think you're right." Dunc pressed his ear to the wood. "I wonder how they opened it."

"Maybe they have a key."

"There's no keyhole. There must be a secret latch or something." He ran his hands lightly back and forth across the wood. "See if you can find anything." Amos and Eddie began searching.

Amos looked through the wine shelves that ran perpendicular to the wall. He ran his fingertips along the little lip on the bottom shelf that kept the bottles from falling off. Nothing.

He did the same with the other shelves. He had to stretch himself out to reach the top. As he did, he smacked something with his leg.

"Ouch!"

He searched the bottom shelf again, more carefully this time.

"It's a faucet."

Dunc knelt down. "Eddie, have you seen any other plumbing in this house?"

"Only in the kitchen."

"Then what's a faucet doing down here?" He turned it on. No water came out.

"Look underneath it," Amos said. "All the dust has been washed away."

Dunc touched the floor. "It's even a little damp. There was water coming out of this not too long ago."

"Why doesn't it work now?" Amos asked.

"I don't know." Dunc turned the faucet handle to off. He sat back and thought hard. After a minute he shrugged his shoulders.

"I can't figure it out. Maybe there's another valve somewhere that you have to turn on first." They looked around for fifteen more minutes. They didn't find anything.

"Too bad you're not a real ghost, Eddie," Amos said. "If you were, you could just stick your head through the wall and see what's on the other side. It would save us a lot of trouble. I wish Blackbeard was here." He stopped. "I take that back."

Then Amos held up his hand. "Listen—do you guys hear anything? Like a sword rattling or something?"

"Be serious, Amos. I'm trying to think."

"I am serious. Do you hear anything?"

A scuffling began very faintly on the other side of the wooden wall, then grew louder and louder. They heard vicious snarls, as if a pack of wild dogs were on the other side.

"What is that?" Dunc cocked his head to hear better.

"I don't know," Amos said, "and I'm not going to wait to find out, either." He was halfway up the stairs in one jump.

"I'm right behind you," Eddie said. He followed him.

Dunc hesitated for a full two count. Then his legs took over, and he was gone.

# **Chapter · 7**

"I don't think this is such a good idea," Amos said. He and Dunc were in his bedroom. Amos was changing out of his school clothes into a pair of jeans and a T-shirt. "These men could be dangerous."

"Maybe."

"I figured out what's behind the door."

"What?"

"Ghost Doberman fang beasts. We get that door open, and they're going to turn us into chili." He sat on the bed, pulling his jeans on over his tennis shoes.

"Why do you do that?" Dunc asked.

"Do what?"

"Put your shoes on before your pants."

"In case there's a fire."

"So?"

"If there's a fire while I'm dressing, I won't have to run out of the house over burning embers barefoot."

"But—" Dunc stopped himself. Sometimes it was best not to try to understand Amos's logic.

Amos had his pants up to his knees when the phone rang. His head popped up.

"Melissa," he said. "That's Melissa's ring."

He almost made it—he came very close. But there were too many things working against him. His jeans were still around his knees. His head was ten feet ahead of his body, thinking of the phone. He threw the door open and ran down the hall.

Except that he couldn't run.

"Amos!" Dunc called. "Pull your pants up!"

Amos looked back over his shoulder. "No time!" he shouted.

Things went from bad to worse at that point.

**48**

As his head was turned, his mother stepped into the hall in front of him, carrying a hamper piled so high with clothes, they hid her face.

"If you have any dirty clothes—"

Amos hit her in the middle like a torpedo, his head down and his feet driving him forward. The hamper flew up in the air and settled upside down perfectly over his shoulders.

It didn't even slow him down.

As he reached the landing his pants slipped down around his ankles and he tripped, completing the disaster and jamming him inside the hamper, which then toppled end over end down the stairs.

Dunc heard him falling and the phone ringing and his mother screaming all at the same time. He ran to the landing.

Amos was at the bottom, packed head-first in the hamper. One arm snaked out of the bottom and groped for the phone on the stand by the door. Instead of the phone, he grabbed a vase. He held it to the side of the hamper opposite his ear.

"Hello?" The phone kept ringing.

"Those are flowers, Amos!" Dunc called down.

"Oh." He dropped the vase, and it shattered on the floor. His hand finally found the phone receiver, and he held it up to the hamper.

"Hello? Hello?"

Amos hung the phone up. He sighed through the woven side of the hamper, his voice muffled. "I let it ring too many times. She hung up."

"Maybe you'll have better luck next time."

"I hope so. I—"

"Amos!" His mother crawled to the landing. A sock hung over her left eye. She was so mad, it looked as if she were going to explode.

"What do you say we go, Dunc?" Amos pushed the hamper off and opened the front door. "I'll be home early, Mom. 'Bye." He was gone before Dunc was halfway down the stairs.

# **Chapter · 8**

From the Rambridge living room, they called Eddie's name several times. No one answered.

"Where is he?" Amos asked.

"I don't know," Dunc said. "Maybe he's taking a nap. Follow me up the stairs. Remember to watch your step."

"Wait a minute, Dunc."

"What?"

"Nothing's going to happen like what happened the last time we climbed the stairs, is it?"

"What do you mean?"

Amos swallowed. He didn't need to say anything more.

"That was only Eddie," Dunc said. "Eddie's not a ghost."

"Oh yeah. When I remember the glowing white and the lantern and the smoking ears, I forget that part."

The hall at the top of the stairs was dark. Amos heard little whispering noises coming from all around him. Or he thought he did.

"What's that?"

"What's what?"

"Listen." He heard them again. "That. What's that?"

"I don't hear anything."

"That," Amos whispered. "Didn't you hear that?"

"You must be hearing mice or something."

"Or something. It's the 'or something' that I'm worried about."

Dunc shook his head. "You've been watching too many scary movies."

"I have not. I haven't seen a scary movie since last night."

**52**

"What was it?"

"*The Creature That Ate the Night*. It was all about this couple that moved into this old house, and they kept hearing noises and—" He stopped. "Oh. I see what you mean."

"Come on. We have to find Eddie."

"Right." Amos followed him down the hall.

They heard music playing from an open door at the end of the hall. When they looked in, they saw Eddie. He was sitting on the floor in front of a battery-operated television eating potato chips. He looked at them and waved.

"Hi, guys."

"Hi, Eddie." Dunc stepped into the room. Amos followed, breathing hard.

"Come on, Eddie," Dunc said. "We have to get down to the cellar."

"Wait until this show is over."

"I want to make sure we're well hidden—"

"Come on—it's over at three thirty. We'll have plenty of time."

Dunc shut the television off. "We have to get going."

They argued for a few minutes, and finally Amos and Dunc had to lead Eddie down the hall.

# Chapter · 9

It was even darker in the cellar than it had been the day before.

Dunc, Amos, and Eddie were hiding behind the wine shelf, back down in a dark corner so full of dust that when they sat down, it rose in clouds around them. Amos sneezed.

"Don't be doing that when they get here," Dunc said. He shined a flashlight in his face.

"It's just the dust. I'll be fine when it settles."

"So what's the plan?" Eddie asked. He gently massaged his ear. He had a small blister on it where the match had burned him.

"We sit and wait and listen."

"Some plan," Amos said.

"What else can we do?"

"Oh, I can think of a lot of things. We could count the ceiling tiles at the court-house, or watch grass grow, or—"

"I mean as far as finding out how to get into the secret room."

"Where the Ghost Doberman fang beasts are waiting. To dismember us."

"Just make sure we're quiet," Eddie said. "If they hear us, we're dead. They'll put us in that room and close the door and—"

Dunc covered Eddie's mouth with one hand and clicked off the flashlight with the other. Someone was fiddling with the lock on the outside door.

The door scraped open. The air by the staircase grew lighter.

"All right, Larry," someone said. "Bring it in here."

Someone else grunted. They heard two sets of footsteps on the other side of the wine shelf.

"Come on, Larry, they're not all that heavy."

"That's easy for you to say. You never have to carry them."

"What's the big deal? They only weigh three pounds each."

"Like I said, that's easy for you to say."

"If it's so heavy, set it on the floor while I do this." Something was set down, and a man groaned. They heard a snarl.

"Vicious little devils, aren't they, Bill?"

"As long as they're in cages, I don't mind."

"I mind."

"Who cares if you mind?"

Larry grunted. "I don't like it here. This place is haunted."

"So? No one bothers us."

"Except ghosts."

"Ghosts only come out at night, Larry. We're never here during the night."

"I don't care. Hurry up. It's too close to night as it is." They heard the sound of splashing water.

The dust around Amos hadn't settled yet, and as soon as whatever was snarling stopped, he felt a tickle in his nose. He put a thumb on each nostril and squeezed tight.

*I'm gonna sneeze. I'm gonna sneeze, and they'll hear us, and the fang beasts will leave us in little quivering strips. . . .*

They heard a metallic click.

"That'll do it," Bill said. The sound of the water stopped. "Bring him inside."

Larry grunted again. They heard foot-steps. Something clicked, then everything was silent. The men seemed to be gone.

Amos couldn't stand it anymore.

He sneezed. He was still pinching his nose, and his eyeballs bugged out as his ears popped. His head expanded like a bal-loon to three times its normal size, and he felt himself beginning to rise off the floor. He opened his mouth, and the excess air rushed out. He collapsed to the floor again.

"I hate that," he whispered. "It's as bad as going outside in the winter with a stuffy nose and having your boogers freeze."

The men outside hadn't heard Amos. Dunc stood and moved around the shelf, stepping carefully.

It was hard to see in the dim light, but

the wall looked the same as it had the day before.

"What was that water sound?" Dunc asked.

"I don't know," Eddie whispered. "Feel under the faucet."

Amos knelt and ran his hand in a circle. "Nothing."

"I don't understand it," Dunc said. "I just don't understand—"

He froze in midsentence. The wall clicked and the whole side of the room began to open.

# Chapter · 10

They were back behind the wine shelf in less time than it takes to think. Amos even went so far as to crawl into the shadows under a shelf in the corner.

"Take care of the water, will you?" Bill asked.

"Sure."

Apparently the men hadn't seen or heard them. They heard a squeaking noise, then the sound of water splashing on the floor.

"I don't care what you say," Larry said. "One of them escaped."

"You're nuts. We only had seven."

"We had eight."

"Seven."

"Eight."

"I'm the boss, and I say we only had seven."

"All right," Larry said. "But I still say that one of them escaped."

"If one did, God help the poor sucker who finds it." The sound of running water stopped.

"Shut it off, and let's get out of here."

"All right." They heard the squeaking sound and footsteps heading toward the door.

It had been dusty where Amos was sitting with Dunc and Eddie before, but now, under the shelf, the dust was so thick, it felt to Amos like a pillow under his head. As he tried to brush it away, he glanced back into the corner.

And almost swallowed his tongue.

Two livid green eyes were staring at him. Big eyes.

*A fang beast,* Amos thought. *An escaped fang beast.*

He tried to stand up. He forgot he was

under the shelf. The sound of his head hitting wood echoed in his ears.

The footsteps stopped. "What was that?" Larry asked.

"What was what?"

"I just heard a noise." One set of footsteps walked back toward the wine shelf.

The green eyes still stared at Amos. He saw a flash of light off something long and white.

Fangs.

*It's going to rip something off me,* Amos thought, *with those fangs. My fingers or my nose or my ears or . . .*

"You're hearing things," Bill said.

"No, I'm not."

"Yes, you are. I'm the boss, and I say you are. Let's go."

"But—"

"I said let's go."

Larry sighed. "All right, but I think—"

"Nobody cares what you think. Let's go." The footsteps moved away. Bill and Larry left and closed the door, still arguing.

*. . . or my chin or my throat.* Amos heard a snarl, then the eyes blinked and

disappeared into a hole in the wall. He scrambled out from beneath the shelf like a crab and grabbed Dunc's arm.

"What's the matter, Amos?"

"Fangs," Amos shook Dunc. "Really, really big, huge, fanged monster—" He pointed back into the corner.

Dunc shined his flashlight under the shelf. "There's nothing down there."

"Are you sure?" Eddie moved two steps away from the corner.

Amos nodded. "I tell you I saw it. Right there." He pointed.

"There're a couple of old bottles under there. Maybe you saw the light reflecting off them."

"Does light snarl?"

"No."

"Then that isn't what I saw."

"There's nothing there now." Dunc shrugged. "We need to figure out how to get into the secret room." He walked back around the wine shelf. Amos followed, watching for the fangs over his shoulder.

"Look," Dunc said. "There's water under

the faucet. There must be another valve. Help me find it."

He crouched and tried to wiggle the faucet and pipe, but they didn't move. He shined his flashlight up into Amos's face.

"Amos, can you—" He stopped. "What's that right next to your head?"

Amos looked. "It's a bottle, just like the one on the other side of my head and the ones by my elbows."

"It's not the same. Look—it has fingerprints all over it."

Amos tried to take the bottle off the shelf. It wouldn't move. "It must be glued down. And there's a hole in the bottom."

Dunc came closer and examined it. "That doesn't make any sense. Why would it be that way?" He frowned. "Unless . . ."

"Unless what?" Amos asked, but Dunc ignored him. He turned to Eddie.

"Do you have any drinking water here?"

"Upstairs, in a canteen."

"Can you get it?"

"Sure. Why?"

"I don't want to say until I know if I'm right."

"I'll be right back." Eddie ran up the cellar stairs. A minute later, he came back down with a canteen in his hand.

"Good," Dunc said. He took the canteen and poured the water into the bottle. It drained down the hole out of sight, and a second later they heard a click. The wooden wall swung slightly toward them.

Amos stared at him. "How did you know that would work?"

"I didn't, but I read an article in the library about something called a water-activated latching mechanism. There's a hidden tube in the wall attached to a lock system. The weight of the water on top of a plate trips the latch. Afterward you have to drain the water off." He reached down and turned the faucet handle. Water gushed out onto the floor. "They used them before electricity to lock secret doors, like this one." He pulled at the door. "Let's see what's on the other side."

"I already know what's on the other side," Amos said. "They're big, with long fangs and green eyes, and they want to take parts of my body off."

But he was speaking to himself. Dunc had already gone through with Eddie behind him. Amos waited. When he didn't hear any ripping sounds or screams of pain, he followed.

Inside was a row of cages with a big, black weasellike animal in each one. Their fur was thick, and their tails were long and bushy.

"I've heard about these," Dunc said. "These are Russian sables."

"Sables?" Eddie asked. "Like in coats?"

"Exactly. They're so valuable and rare, the Russian government won't let them be exported out of the country. Larry and Bill must be sable smugglers."

"They look so cute," Amos said. "Say, you don't suppose that's what I saw? The fangs? They don't look so dangerous." He put his finger to one of the cages. The sable made a spit-hissing sound and hit the end of the finger like a buzz saw.

"Ow!" He hugged his almost-devoured finger to his chest.

"So what do we do now?" Eddie asked.

"I guess we go to the authorities. We'll tell them—"

The click of the lock on the outside of the basement door stopped him.

"They're back." Amos tried to whisper, but it came out a squeak. "The smablers. I mean, the snuggles. . . ."

The door opened before he could say more, before they could run or even move, and the three were caught flat-footed standing in the room with the sables by Bill and Larry.

# Chapter · 11

"What's going on here?" Bill demanded.

Nobody replied.

"When I tell you to run," Dunc whispered in Amos's ear, "run."

"Where to?" Amos asked, but Dunc didn't answer him. Instead he snapped off his flashlight.

"Run."

Larry was reaching for Amos just as the darkness closed down. There was one moment, one part of a second, when everything seemed to stop, to hang in the air.

Then the world went insane.

The tiny room exploded silently in a

green-blue light that seemed to come from inside everybody, shooting beams out of Larry's eyes and mouth, out of Dunc's ears and bouncing off the walls, into and out of the cages and sables, whipping back and forth and getting brighter and brighter until everything—people, walls, floor, everything—glowed and flowed.

"What . . . ?"

Small things moved around the room, flying, zipping back and forth. They were tiny, and when one of them stopped on Amos's shoulder, he turned to see a little fat person sitting there, not four inches high. It was dressed in a little pirate suit and carrying a little pirate sword, and it grinned and jumped at Larry and was gone before Amos really knew it was there.

With other small figures it flew through the green light, around and around, unhooking all the cages and letting the sables loose, unbuttoning and unzipping the clothes on Bill and Larry so their pants dropped around their ankles. The sables exploded from the cages and were soon running around the room chasing the little zip-ping people.

All in seconds, tiny seconds.

"I don't like this," Larry said, as if by looking at his face no one could see that.

"I had an uncle once," Amos started, "who, before he overdosed, used to talk about things like this in the sixties . . ." It was as far as he got.

The green light and all the little people vanished. It was dark for only a moment.

*"Who disturbs my sleep?"*

A new white flashing, searing light tore the room apart. Standing next to them, over them, towering so his head hit the ceiling, was Blackbeard.

There were matches in his hair, in his ears, under his hat; his eyes were on fire, burning deep and intensely red. When he opened his mouth, flames shot out and streamed toward Larry and Bill.

*"Burn,"* Blackbeard cried, a cry from all the dead who ever were. *"You will burn for-ever."*

He waved an arm, and when it came up Amos—who felt as if he had turned inside

71

out—saw that the hand held a cutlass with a blade of fire.

It cut through Larry and Bill and seemed to slice them in half. It threw them back out of the small room into the main part of the cellar and dumped them by the door in a heap.

Then it was over.

The room was again dark, totally dark.

"Dunc?" Amos squeaked. "Are you there?"

Silence.

"Dunc? *Dunc?*"

"Over here."

"Are you all right?"

"I'm trying to get the light to work." He thumped it against his leg, and a flashlight beam filled the room.

Larry and Bill were still on the floor in the other room. The sables were tearing around, in and out of the open door.

"What happened?" Eddie asked.

"Dunc—" Amos squeaked.

"Come on," Dunc said. "We have to tie those two up before they come around."

"Dunc—" Amos squeaked again.

"What?"

"I peed my pants."

Dunc looked at him. "Jeez, no kidding. What have you been doing, saving it up for a week?"

"I'm sorry."

"That's all right. Sometimes even brave people pee their pants when they're frightened."

"Aren't you scared?" Amos asked. "Didn't you see all that?"

"Sure. But we still have to tie them up, then get the cops."

"It was ghosts," Amos said. He swallowed loudly. "It was a whole bunch of ghosts, and one of them sat on my shoulder, and Dunc, you don't even seem to care."

"Sure I care. But let's tie these two guys up before they cause trouble, then get the cops. Then we can talk."

Amos still hadn't moved. Dunc found some electrical cord and tied Larry and Bill hands to feet, and then back to back together, and Amos still hadn't moved.

"It was Blackbeard," he said. "He was

ten feet tall, and he had a sword a mile long."

Dunc came back. He took Amos by the hand and led him out into the main part of the cellar. "Yeah, it was Blackbeard."

Amos looked at Bill and Larry as if he were seeing them for the first time.

"Their hair is white."

Dunc nodded.

"Even their eyebrows."

"They were kind of scared. Now let's get the police."

"Blackbeard could have done the same thing to us," Amos said.

"But he didn't. He—" Dunc stopped, looking suddenly at Eddie. "Eddie, your feet are sunk into the floor."

Eddie looked down. "Oops." Without appearing to move, he floated up a few inches. "You weren't supposed to see that."

Dunc stuttered. "You—"

Eddie sighed. "It just gets so *tiring* having to scare people away all the time. I wanted someone else to do it for a change. When I saw you wouldn't be able to, I had to do something."

"Eddie," Amos said. "Eddie the teacher. Edward Teach." He swallowed. "B-B-B-B . . ."

He stopped, caught his breath, and tried again. "B-B-B-B . . ."

"Blackbeard," Dunc completed for him. He took a step backward. "Why aren't Amos and I scared stiff like these two are?"

"I didn't slice you with this." Eddie took a four-foot flaming sword out from behind his back. "And I don't want to. I do have a treasure to guard, though, and you are in my house. So if you don't mind—" He waved the sword once through the air.

"Enough said." Dunc took Amos by the arm. "We're on our way out."

"Have the police come pick these two up, if you don't mind," Eddie said.

"No problem."

"B-B-B-B . . ." Amos repeated. He was too frightened to move.

Dunc finally had to open the basement door and push Amos out—his feet leaving skid marks in the dust—before he could run next door and call the police.

# **Chapter · 12**

Amos sat on the end of Dunc's bed and rubbed his leg. "I almost broke it this time."

"What happened?" Dunc was working on a scale model of a diplodocus. He was painting the skin to match the color on the box the model came in.

"It's because of Eddie," Amos said.

"But Eddie made you famous—at least for a day."

"I just wish the TV people had delayed the interview until after I had changed my pants."

"Yeah. Too bad." He flicked his paintbrush. "This diplodocus will look great next to my triceratops."

"When we were in the paper," Amos said, "and they took my picture, I was sure Melissa would call."

"Especially after you dedicated the smugglers' capture to her," Dunc said, nodding. "That was almost perfect."

"It wasn't much of a capture. It's been three weeks, and I heard a cop at the drugstore say they still haven't moved. They have them propped in a corner of the cell, and they just stand there."

"They were pretty scared." Dunc pointed a paintbrush at Amos's leg. "You still haven't told me about the leg."

"Oh. After the story was in the paper and on television, I was sure Melissa would call, and I was dead right. Friday night I was sitting alone in my room when I heard the phone downstairs. So I made my move. You know, you have to hit by that all-important second ring, or they lose interest."

"Lose interest." Dunc nodded.

"So I cleared my room in record time and

hit the stairs with good form—almost classic."

"Good form." Dunc used two hands to steady the brush. There was a tiny part around the diplodocus's eyes where it was hard to paint.

"I had it. It was a straight shot down the stairs, two jumps across the living room—that's all I had to make."

"And then?" Dunc said, nodding.

"And then my sister's gerbil—"

"Gerbil?"

"Yeah. It escaped from its cage somehow, and when I stepped on it at the top of the stairs—"

"You stepped on a gerbil?"

"Sort of. When I felt something soft, I tried not to step on it, but that threw my pace off. I dived over the railing on the landing. I thought I was a goner, but luckily I had my shoes double-tied. My shoelace loop caught on the ornamental ball at the top of the staircase as I flew over, and I wound up hanging upside down from the railing until Mom came home from work."

"How long was that?"

"About two hours."

"You hung upside down for two hours?"

"That's how I hurt my leg."

"So you never reached the phone."

"No. But it was Melissa—I could tell from the ring."

"Amos . . ."

"I'm going to take it easy," Amos said, leaning back against the wall. "Not push it and ask her to marry me right away."

"Amos . . ."

"I should try to buy a home first, don't you think?"

"Amos . . ."

"Or maybe a trailer house."

"Amos . . ."

keep them from retrieving the valuable missing doll?

### Culpepper's Cannon

Dunc and Amos are researching the Civil War cannon that stands in the town square when they find a note inside telling them about a time portal. Entering it through the dressing room of La Petite, a women's clothing store, the boys find themselves in downtown Chatham on March 8, 1862—the day before the historic clash between the *Monitor* and the *Merrimac*. But the Confederate soldiers they meet mistake them for Yankee spies. Will they make it back to the future in one piece?

### Dunc Gets Tweaked

Best friends Dunc and Amos meet up with a new buddy named Lash when they enter the radical world of skateboard competition. When somebody "cops"—steals—Lash's prototype skateboard, the boys are determined to get it back. After all, Lash is about to shoot for a totally rad world's record! Along the way they learn a major lesson: *Never* kiss a monkey!

### Dunc's Halloween

Dunc and his best friend, Amos, are planning the best route to get the most candy on Halloween. But their plans change when Amos is slightly bitten by a werewolf. He begins scratching himself and chasing UPS trucks: he's become a werepuppy!

### Dunc Breaks the Record

Best-friends-for-life Dunc and Amos have a small problem when they try hang gliding— they crash in the wilderness. Luckily Amos has read a book about a boy who survived in the wilderness for fifty-four days. Too bad Amos doesn't have a hatchet. Things go from bad to worse when a wild man holds the boys captive. Can anything save them now?

### Amos Gets Famous

Deciphering a code they find in a library book, best-friends-for-life Amos and Dunc stumble on to a burglary ring. The burglars' next target is the home of Melissa, the girl of Amos's dreams (who doesn't even know that he's alive). Amos longs to be a hero to

Melissa, so nothing will stop him from solving this case—not even a mind-boggling collision with a jock, a chimpanzee, and a toilet.